the CRiTTeR club

Ellie and the Good-Luck Pig

by Callie Barkley ♥ illustrated by Marsha Riti

LITTLE SIMON

New York London Toronto Sydney New Delhi

 LITTLE SIMON

An imprint of Simon & Schuster Children's Publishing Division • 1230 Avenue of the Americas, New York, New York 10020 • First Little Simon paperback edition February 2015 • Copyright © 2015 by Simon & Schuster, Inc. All rights reserved, including the right of reproduction in whole or in part in any form. LITTLE SIMON is a registered trademark of Simon & Schuster, Inc., and associated colophon is a trademark of Simon & Schuster, Inc. For information about special discounts for bulk purchases, please contact Simon & Schuster Special Sales at 1-866-506-1949 or business@simonandschuster.com. The Simon & Schuster Speakers Bureau can bring authors to your live event. For more information or to book an event contact the Simon & Schuster Speakers Bureau at 1-866-248-3049 or visit our website at www.simonspeakers.com. Designed by Laura Roode. The text of this book was set in ITC Stone Informal Std.
Manufactured in the United States of America 0316 MTN   10 9 8 7 6 5
Library of Congress Cataloging-in-Publication Data
Barkley, Callie. Ellie and the good-luck pig / by Callie Barkley ; illustrated by Marsha Riti.   First edition. pages cm. — (The Critter Club ; #10) Summary: After winning the lead role in a play, acing a spelling test, and finding money, second-grader Ellie wonders if the Critter Club animal shelter's newest animal—a little pink pig—is bringing her good luck. [1. Animal shelters—Fiction. 2. Pigs—Fiction. 3. Luck—Fiction. 4. Friendship—Fiction.] I. Riti, Marsha, illustrator. II. Title. PZ7.B250585El 2015 [Fic]—dc23 2014043208
ISBN 978-1-4814-2403-5 (hc)
ISBN 978-1-4814-2402-8 (pbk)
ISBN 978-1-4814-2404-2 (eBook)

Table of Contents

The New Guest

Ellie checked her sparkly red watch. "Ms. Sullivan," she said, "what time are they coming again?"

Ms. Sullivan laughed. "Like I said the last time you asked—any minute!"

Ellie sighed. "But that was at least two minutes ago!"

This time Amy, Liz, and Marion

laughed, too. The four girls and Ms. Sullivan were in front of The Critter Club, the animal shelter they ran in Ms. Sullivan's barn. They were waiting to welcome Plum, their newest animal guest.

"Do we have the food ready for her?" Marion asked.

Amy nodded. "My mom says Plum eats all kinds of fruits and vegetables." Amy's mom was a veterinarian. She helped out with the animals at The Critter Club.

"She also said they are very social animals. We should make sure one of us can come here to play with her every day."

Liz knelt down to pet Ms. Sullivan's dog. "I wonder what *you'll* think of Plum, Rufus."

Just then, Rufus started to bark, but not at Liz. He was barking at the road. Everyone looked that way. A pickup truck was pulling in to Ms. Sullivan's driveway.

"She's here! She's here!" Ellie exclaimed. She jumped and clapped. They'd had all kinds of animals at The Critter Club: kittens, bunnies, turtles, even frogs. But never an animal like Plum!

The pickup truck came to a stop in front of the barn. A smiling young lady with short, dark hair hopped out. "Hi, girls! Hello, Ms. Sullivan!" she said.

"Hi, Anna!" they all replied.

They had met her the day before when she'd come to check out The Critter Club. Ellie felt so happy and proud that Anna had decided it was a good place for Plum—at least for the time being.

Anna walked around to the back of the pickup. "So are you ready to meet Plum?" she asked.

"Yes!" the girls cried.

Ellie could see the top of a large metal crate in the back of the truck. Anna climbed up and brought it down to the ground.

Inside was the cutest, pinkest, littlest pig Ellie had ever seen!

"Plum!" Ellie squealed. She knelt

down beside the crate and peered between the slats. "I'm so excited to meet you!" Plum began to make her own high-pitched pig squeals. She turned around and around in a circle. "And *you* seem excited to come out!" Ellie added.

"I'm so glad you offered to find

a home for her," Anna said as she opened the crate. "Plum has had only our tiny backyard to roam in. She needs more space!"

All of a sudden, Plum rocketed out of the crate. In a flash she was off. Rufus chased her, barking playfully. The two of them ran around and around the barn. Anna, the girls, and Ms. Sullivan looked on and smiled.

"Yep!" said Ellie. "Space is one thing we definitely have at The Critter Club!"

chapter 2

Lunch-Table Talk

The next day Ellie, Liz, Marion, and Amy sat together at lunch. It was a Monday at Santa Vista Elementary School, where the girls were in the same second-grade class.

"Busy weekend, huh?" Ellie said as she unpacked her lunch.

The girls had spent Sunday afternoon playing with Plum. They

had also helped Ms. Sullivan start to dig Plum's wallow—a mud pit for her to roll around in. Then Ellie had run off to audition for a play at a local kids' theater.

"How did your audition go?" Liz asked.

Ellie got goose bumps on her arms. "I think it went really well!" she said hopefully. "I tried out for the lead. A lot of other kids did too. But maybe I have a shot."

Liz squeezed Ellie's arm. "I bet you'll get it!" she said.

Amy shared some news from her dad, a newspaper editor. "He's going to put an ad in the paper about Plum," Amy said. "Maybe someone will read it and want to adopt her." All the girls agreed that was a great idea.

Liz told her friends about a painting she had worked on over the weekend. "It's going to be a birthday present for my aunt," Liz explained. "She *loves* pigs! So I used my memory of Plum to help me paint."

Marion sighed. "Well, I spent most of Saturday doing homework. Can you believe Mrs. Sienna scheduled that spelling test for today—a *Monday*?"

The spelling test!

Ellie groaned. "Oh, no! Nana Gloria quizzed me a little on Saturday. But we only got through about half of the words. And yesterday there was so much going on. I forgot to finish studying!"

Ellie wasn't hungry anymore. She had gotten hundreds on the last three spelling tests. *Looks like that's over!* she thought. *What a way to start the week.*

Spelling tests were always right after lunch. Back in the classroom, Mrs. Sienna passed out the lined paper. Ellie took a deep breath. She knew one bad spelling grade wasn't the end of the world. But she also knew Nana Gloria would ask how she'd done.

Contractions
do + not
= don't
can + not
= can't

Chapter 3

Mostly Perfect Monday

Ellie beamed as her mom drove her to The Critter Club after school that day. She looked down at the paper in her lap. It said "100."

Ellie almost couldn't believe it. She had known how to spell a lot of the words. But there were some she hadn't been sure about at all.

I can't wait to show Nana Gloria,

she thought. She gazed out the rain-splattered window. *Now if only it would stop raining!*

All four girls were meeting up at The Critter Club. They had planned to play outside with Plum. But it had been raining all day.

Ellie's mom pulled up to Ms.

Sullivan's barn. "Marion's dad will drive you home at five," her mom reminded her.

"Okay!" replied Ellie. She put up the hood of her raincoat. Then she stepped out of the car and closed the door.

As she did, the rain let up—then stopped. Ellie put down her hood to make sure. No more raindrops! She smiled and looked up at the sky. The sun was just peeking out from behind a huge gray cloud.

"Wow! Great timing!" she said.

Ellie hurried inside to find Amy, Liz, and Marion already there. They were watching Plum poke around in her food trough. "Hey, guess what!" Ellie called to them. "The rain stopped."

"Hooray!" cried Liz.

"How about we see if Plum likes her wallow?" Amy suggested.

Leading Plum outside, the girls

squinted in the bright sunshine.

"Look!" Marion said, pointing up at the sky. Ellie looked up. A bright, clear rainbow stretched across the misty sky!

The dreary, rainy day had turned into the most perfect sunny afternoon.

The girls led Plum over to the hole they had dug for her.

"How convenient!"

said Ellie. "The rain filled it up."

Amy nodded. "It's the perfect muddy mess," she said. "What do you think, Plum?"

Plum wasted no time. She plunged herself into the wallow, splashing mud everywhere. The

girls laughed, watching
her roll around—
until Plum decided she wanted
to come out. Ellie shrieked as the
mud-covered piglet came running
straight at them. Plum seemed to

think it was a game. She chased Ellie around Ms. Sullivan's yard as Ellie half-shrieked, half-laughed.

Finally, Liz managed to catch the pig. Together they hosed Plum

off. Soon she was squeaky clean.

Tired out, the girls found a patch of sun-dried grass and sat down to enjoy the sunshine. Plum plopped down next to them.

"Oooh! Clover!" said Liz, sitting next to Ellie. She pointed to a clover patch between them.

"Hmm," said Ellie. "I wonder if there's a four-leaf clover in here somewhere!" It *had* been a pretty perfect afternoon. Maybe Ellie would find a lucky clover to really top it off. But she didn't.

Later, Ellie got a ride home from The Critter Club with Marion and

her dad. As Ellie entered the house, her mom came out from the kitchen to meet her.

"Hi, Mom!" said Ellie. "Where's Nana Gloria? I want to show her my . . ." Ellie's voice trailed off. She noticed the look on her mom's face. It was her bad-news face. "What is it? What's the matter?"

"Let's go out to the porch," Mrs. Mitchell said. She sat down on the staircase. Ellie sat next to her.

"The play director called," her mom said gently. "I'm sorry, honey, but you didn't get the lead."

"Oh," Ellie managed to say. She shrugged. "That's okay." But a lump was rising in her throat.

"I know," her mom said, pulling her close. "You really wanted that part. But there is *some* good news: You got the role of the teacher. That one has lots of lines, right?"

Ellie nodded. "Right," she said. But it wasn't the lead.

The afternoon hadn't turned out so perfectly after all.

Chapter 4

Good-News Tuesday

Ellie moped her way through school on Tuesday. She couldn't stop thinking about the part she *hadn't* gotten.

Ellie didn't even enjoy music class, which was usually her favorite. It reminded her of the play, which was a musical.

And she loved her teacher, Mrs. Sienna. But today the teacher

reminded Ellie of the smaller role she would be playing.

Ellie wasn't even all that excited about going to The Critter Club after school with Amy. She had told her friends at lunch that she hadn't gotten the lead. She was worried

Amy might bring it up. Ellie didn't feel like talking about it.

When the last bell rang, Ellie met up with Amy outside. "My mom is parked over there," Amy said, pointing. Ellie saw Dr. Purvis' minivan in the pickup circle. It was easy to spot with SANTA VISTA VET CLINIC written on the side in purple letters.

Santa Vista Vet Clinic

Then Ellie spotted her own mom parked right behind Dr. Purvis. Mrs. Mitchell and Dr. Purvis were standing together on the curb.

They were both waving at Ellie and Amy.

Ellie ran over. "Mom, did you forget?" she said. "I'm going to

The Critter Club with Amy and her mom today."

Mrs. Mitchell had a huge smile on her face. "I know," she replied. "But I have some news. I had to come tell you!"

"Really?" Ellie asked. "What? What?!" She figured it must be really good if her mom couldn't wait until she got home.

Mrs. Mitchell explained. "Well, the play director called again. She said that the girl who was offered the lead can't take it. The director

says the part is yours . . . *if* you still want it!"

Ellie's jaw dropped open. She couldn't believe it! "Of course I still want it!" she cried. "It's all I thought about all day long! Woo-hooooo!"

Amy laughed and cheered with

Ellie. "Congratulations!" Amy said, hugging her friend.

"I'm so happy for you, Ellie!" said Dr. Purvis. "Come on! We can go tell Ms. Sullivan the good news too!"

At The Critter Club, Ms. Sullivan was just as thrilled for Ellie as everyone else. "That's wonderful!" she cried. Then she leaned in close to

Ellie and whispered, "Ruby Fairchild knows you'll be great!"

She winked at Ellie. Ellie smiled— she was the only person in town who knew that Ms. Sullivan had once been a famous movie actress named Ruby Fairchild.

"Oh! Before I forget," Ms. Sullivan added, "you left your raincoat here yesterday, Ellie." Ms. Sullivan pointed to a red slicker hanging on a wall hook. "The weather was so nice when you left, it's no wonder you forgot it."

"Thanks, Ms. Sullivan!" Ellie replied. "I'll put it on to help clean out Plum's pen."

She went over and put on her raincoat. "Okay, Plum! I'm ready for you!" she announced, and thrust her hands into her pockets.

Right away, her left hand felt something. She pulled it out and held it up.

It was a five-dollar bill! "Wait," said Ellie. "Where did this come from?"

Ms. Sullivan shrugged.

Amy asked, "Isn't it yours?"

But Ellie didn't remember putting five dollars in that pocket.

Wow, thought Ellie. *Finding a penny is pretty lucky. Finding five dollars? That's got to be really, really lucky!*

Chapter 5

String of Luck

That night Ellie lay awake in bed. She was thinking back over her week. It had been pretty great so far. First, The Critter Club had gotten a fun new guest. Then Ellie had aced her Monday spelling test. And she hadn't even studied all the words! Later that day, the weather had cleared at just the right time.

And then, she had gotten the lead in the play *and* found the money in her pocket!

I've been really lucky, thought Ellie. *And it all started with Plum. . . .*

Ellie gasped. Could it be? Was Plum bringing her good luck?

The idea bounced around in her tired brain. Soon she drifted off to sleep. She had a dream. She was starring in a Broadway play that got rave reviews. Plum was waving from the audience.

In the morning Ellie decided not to tell anyone about her idea that

Plum was a good-luck pig. For one thing, she felt silly saying it out loud. For another, well, what if it *was* true? She didn't want to jinx it by talking about it!

So Ellie tried to go about her week as usual. But it wasn't a usual week.

On Wednesday morning she won a class raffle. The prize was an extra half hour of reading time while the rest of the class was cleaning out their cubbies. Somehow, Ellie was not very surprised she'd won.

On Thursday she climbed the rope fastest during gym class—faster than the strongest kids in her class. Ellie figured luck just wasn't on their side. *Unlike me!* she thought.

On Friday morning Ellie was having breakfast when the phone rang. Her mom answered. When she hung up,

she told Ellie, "That was the dentist's office. Your appointment for today has to be pushed back to next month."

Ellie just poured milk in her

cereal and whispered, "Thank you, Plum."

Walking into school later, Ellie wondered what luck the day would bring! As she slid into her seat, Amy

came hurrying into the classroom.
She saw Ellie and went right over.

"Guess what?" Amy said. "I have
the *best* news!"

Ellie sat up straight in her chair
and smiled. *Here we go!* she thought.

This should be good! She couldn't wait to hear what Amy had to say.

"Someone called about Plum!" Amy went on. "They saw the ad in my dad's newspaper. They want to meet Plum—and maybe even adopt her!"

Ellie's face fell . . . and her heart sank.

Chapter 6

Mr. Fisk's Farm

"Isn't this all happening a little fast?" Ellie asked Amy, Liz, and Marion.

The girls had gathered at The Critter Club on Saturday morning. The man who had called about Plum was coming to visit—any minute. Liz was hosing Plum down for the third time that morning.

Every time she got the piglet clean, Plum ran off and jumped in the wallow again.

"I mean, who is this man?" Ellie went on. "What do we know about him, anyway?"

"Well," said Amy, "Dad says his name is Mr. Fisk. He owns a farm sanctuary in Springfield—about ten minutes away."

"I've heard of those!" said Marion. "It's like a rescue shelter for farm animals—except the animals get to stay there for the rest of their lives."

"Right!" said Amy. "And I guess Mr. Fisk has lots of animals: cows, chickens, goats, even other pigs!"

Liz pet Plum's head. "Hear that, Plum? Other pigs!"

Marion added, "It sounds perfect!"

Ellie wrinkled her brow. It *did* sound pretty perfect. But she didn't want to say so. She didn't want Plum to go!

Just then, a car turned in to the driveway. Ms. Sullivan came outside to join the girls as an older man in a flannel shirt got out of the car.

"Hello," he said. "I'm Mr. Fisk. I called about Plum the pig."

"Hi, Mr. Fisk," Ms. Sullivan said. "We were expecting you."

"Welcome to The Critter Club!" said Liz.

"We're so excited you might want to adopt Plum!" said Marion.

"Would you like to meet her?" Amy asked.

"Yes, please, I would!" Mr. Fisk replied.

Ellie didn't say a word. She just followed as the others led the way into the barn.

"Oh, what a beautiful piglet!" Mr. Fisk said when he spotted Plum in her pen.

The girls gathered around to tell him a little about Plum.

"She's shy at first," said Amy. "But once she gets to know you, she's so sweet."

Marion said, "She loves the mud! But she doesn't mind being hosed off so she's nice and clean."

Next, Liz chimed in. "Her favorite color is blue." All the girls gave Liz a puzzled look. "At least, I *think* it is," Liz added.

Everyone laughed. Everyone except for Ellie. She felt like it was her turn to say something. But what?

Then Ellie had an idea. What if she said something *bad* about Plum? *That way, Mr. Fisk won't want to take her,* Ellie thought, *and Plum can stay!*

Good-bye, Plum

Ellie opened her mouth to speak. Mr. Fisk turned to listen. He was watching her, waiting. . . .

Finally, Ellie blurted out, "I'll—I mean *we'll* really miss her."

She couldn't do it. She couldn't say anything bad about Plum. She was such a sweet pig. And deep down, Ellie knew Plum would be

75

happy at Mr. Fisk's farm sanctuary. The rest of the morning was a blur for Ellie. Mr. Fisk went home to get his animal trailer. He returned a little while later to take Plum to her new home.

Before Mr. Fisk loaded Plum into the trailer, the girls and Ms. Sullivan said their good-byes. When it was Ellie's turn, she leaned in close to the pig's fuzzy pink ear.

"Thanks for the good luck, Plum," she whispered. "And good luck to you at your new place."

Plum looked Ellie in the eye and snorted a few times.

Then the girls and Ms. Sullivan waved as Mr. Fisk drove off. Ellie stood there the longest, watching them go.

"Come on, Ellie!" Liz called. "Want to ride home with us?"

Ellie looked over toward the barn door. Liz, Marion, and Amy had their bikes out and their helmets on. Ellie hurried to catch up.

Halfway home, Marion swerved around a big pothole on the bike path. "Look out!" she called to the other girls behind her. But it was

too late. Liz hit the pothole but kept going. Amy hit it and cycled on.

Then Ellie hit it—and she heard a loud pop. She stopped and got off her bike to check it out.

Her front tire was flat.

"Oh, no," Ellie groaned. With

Plum gone, she *thought* her good luck might be over. But maybe it was worse than that.

Maybe the *bad* luck was about to begin.

Ellie woke up on Sunday morning and decided to think more positively. "Ellie," she said aloud to herself, "you're being silly. Who has ever heard of a good-luck pig?"

Later she made popovers with Nana Gloria. Usually, they puffed up in the oven—hollow on the

inside, golden brown on the out-side. Today they rose halfway, then fell sadly.

"That's funny," Nana Gloria said. "Did we forget the baking soda?"

Ellie didn't think so, but she tried to just let it go. Now and then, these things happened.

In the afternoon Ellie and her little brother, Toby, took their dog, Sam, for a walk. A rabbit jumped out of a bush in front of Sam. Sam

strained at the leash, yanking it out of Ellie's hand. Sam darted off after the rabbit. It took Ellie and Toby an hour to chase him down.

Okay, thought Ellie. *That felt like bad luck.* But Sam was always trying to chase rabbits and squirrels. This time probably had *nothing* to do with Plum leaving. Right?

The Blues

"All right, class!" Mrs. Sienna announced Monday morning. "Clear your desks and take out a pencil. We are having a pop math quiz on symmetry."

The whole class groaned, Ellie loudest of all. She hated pop quizzes. They made her nervous. Then it was hard to concentrate.

Mrs. Sienna hardly ever gave pop quizzes. "Why today?" Ellie whispered to Amy in the row next to her. Amy shrugged.

Ellie had a feeling she knew the answer: bad luck!

Mrs. Sienna passed out the quiz

papers. Ellie looked down. The sheet was filled with shapes.

Ellie thought hard, trying to remember: How did you know if a shape was symmetrical or not?

She looked at each of the shapes.

Circle the shapes that are symmetrical. Draw the lines of symmetry on the symmetrical shapes.

The longer she looked at them, the more nervous she got. Then slowly, slowly, the shapes on the page seemed to change. Now they all looked like . . . pigs!

Circle the shapes that are symmetrical. Draw the lines of symmetry on the symmetrical shapes.

Ellie knew she had to calm down. She took a deep breath. She tried her best, finished the quiz, and handed in her paper.

But she felt terrible. Ellie knew she hadn't done well at all.

The rest of the morning wasn't so great either. It was gym day and Ellie didn't have her sneakers.

"I'm sorry, Mrs. Payne," Ellie said to the gym teacher. "I forgot. I was so excited about wearing my brand-new dress. And these shoes match so well."

Mrs. Payne smiled warmly. "It *is* a lovely dress, Ellie," she said, "and I love your shoes. But you know the rules. Only sneakers on the gym floor. You'll have to

sit on the bleachers today."

Finally lunchtime rolled around. Ellie hoped a little time with her friends would make her feel better.

She opened her lunchbox and pulled out her juice box. She tried to poke the straw through, but it wouldn't go in. She grasped the juice box tighter and tried again, and again, and—

"Aaaaaaaaaaaaah!" Ellie cried. The straw was in. But her tight grip on the juice box sprayed juice through the straw—and all over Ellie.

She jumped up and looked down at her dress. It was splattered all over with red fruit-punch spots.

Ellie couldn't hold it in any longer. The pop quiz, the forgotten sneakers, and now this!

"My new dress!" she cried. "It's ruined! *And it's all Mr. Fisk's fault!*"

Ellie Talks It Out

Liz, Amy, and Marion stared at Ellie. They looked very confused.

"Did you just say it's Mr. Fisk's fault?" asked Amy.

"The fruit punch on your dress?" added Liz.

"What does Mr. Fisk have to do with it?" said Marion.

Ellie sat back down. She looked

at her friends. She was tired of keep-
ing things to herself. So she decided
to tell them everything.

"Well, I don't really mean that
it's Mr. Fisk's fault," she began. "It's
just . . . I think Plum was bringing
me good luck. Now she's gone. And
so is my good luck!"

She reminded the girls about the
spelling test and sudden weather
change on Monday. She'd gotten
the lead in the play and found the
money on Tuesday. "And then I
won that raffle, climbed the rope
the fastest in gym, and had my

dentist appointment moved to a different day!"

"Wow!" Liz exclaimed. "You really *did* have some good luck last week!"

Ellie nodded. "I know!"

The girls were quiet for a few moments. Then Amy spoke up. "But you didn't just have good *luck*," she said.

Ellie tilted her head to one side. "What do you mean?"

"Ellie, you're an amazing speller," Amy said. "Haven't you gotten one hundreds on the last three spelling tests? You've learned a lot of spelling rules. Maybe you're just a natural!"

Ellie thought about it. It seemed to make sense.

"And they must have loved you during your play audition," added Marion. "That's why they called you to sub in."

"And in gym," said Liz, "you've always been super speedy. None of us can ever catch you in tag!"

Ellie took a bite of her sandwich.
She was letting their words sink in.

"Okay," she said at last, "but then why am I the only one who got a flat tire yesterday? Liz and Amy hit the pothole too."

Marion smiled. "I have an idea about that," she said. "We three filled

our tires with air at Ms. Sullivan's,
right after Plum left."

"Oh . . ." Ellie said, remembering
how she'd stood by the driveway for
a while. She'd been so upset about
Plum, she hadn't noticed what the
girls were doing.

"Then what about today?" Ellie said. "I forgot my gym shoes, ruined my dress, and did terribly on that quiz!"

Amy nodded. "Yeah. Those first two do seem like bad luck."

"Just plain old everyday bad luck," Marion agreed.

Liz leaned over the table toward Ellie. "But guess what?" she said. "I didn't do well on that quiz either."

"Me neither," said Amy.

"Neither did I!" said Marion. "Nobody was ready for it!"

Ellie's face brightened. "Really?" she said.

Her friends nodded their heads and smiled.

"So Plum wasn't a good-luck pig?" Ellie asked.

The girls all shook their heads.

"And now that she's gone, I won't have bad luck forever?" Ellie asked.

"Nope!" said Liz.

"Uh-uh," said Amy.

"No way," said Marion.

Ellie beamed. "Yes!" she cried. "I think you're right!" All of a sudden, she felt so much better!

In celebration, Ellie grabbed her lunchbox and threw it into the air. "Yippee!" she cried, reaching out to catch it on the way down.

But she had forgotten that she hadn't zipped the lunchbox. A napkin, a banana, and half a sandwich fell out. They landed on Ellie's head. She frowned.

Then all four friends burst out laughing.

Clover All Over

A few days later, after school, the girls met at The Critter Club. They had to get the barn ready for two new guests! A family was going on vacation. The Critter Club girls were going to take care of their hamster and their dog while they were away.

After they finished their jobs, they went to sit in the clover patch.

"What do you think Plum is doing right now?" Ellie asked.

Liz giggled. "She's either getting muddy or getting hosed off!"

The girls all laughed. "Good one, Liz," Ellie said, patting her on the back. As she did, Ellie's sparkly red watch fell off. It dropped into the clover patch.

Ellie reached to pick it up and—

Could it be? Ellie looked closer.

Under the watch, in the exact spot where it landed, was a four-leaf clover!

"Oh! Look! Look!" she cried, pointing it out to Liz, Amy, and Marion. "That is just so *lucky*—" Ellie stopped herself. "I mean," she said, "I guess I must have really good eyesight!"

Read on for a sneak peek at
the next Critter Club book:

Liz and the
Sand-Castle Contest

Liz Jenkins peered through the glass side of the fish tank. "I really wish I were a fish right now!" she said.

She and her friends, Ellie, Amy, and Marion, were at The Critter Club. They were standing around an aquarium filled with colorful fish. The girls were pet sitting the fish for a couple of weeks.

"It *would* feel great to go for a swim," Ellie agreed. "Do you think fish *ever* get hot?"

Santa Vista was in the middle of a summer heat wave. Liz would bet it was about ninety-five degrees in Ms. Sullivan's barn. It was the headquarters of The Critter Club, the animal rescue shelter the girls had started.

"I forgot how hot it can get here," Marion said. She had just returned from horseback riding camp. "Up in the mountains at camp, it was so cool!"

Amy sighed. "I'm just glad my writing program is inside," she said. "The classroom at the rec center is super air-conditioned!"

Amy sprinkled fish food into the water. The fish raced up to the surface to snatch the crumbs.

"You're lucky," Ellie said to Amy. "Nana Gloria doesn't like turning on the air conditioner." Nana Gloria was Ellie's grandmother. She lived with Ellie's family. "I'm going to melt by the time my parents get back from their trip!" She turned to Liz. "You have to take me with you to Luna Beach tomorrow!"

Liz giggled. "I wish I could take all three of you!" she replied. "But our car is going to be packed!"

Liz's family was leaving the next day. They had rented a beach cottage for a long weekend. Liz could not wait. Even when it was hot at the beach, there were sea breezes and cool waves. Liz was a strong swimmer. She could body surf all weekend to stay cool.

Liz looked down at the fish. "I'm just sorry I won't be able to help with these guys," Liz said.

If you like **the CRITTER club** you'll love **HEIDI HECKELBECK**